Gigi and Lulu's
GIGANTIC
FIGHT

Pamela Duncan Edwards • Illustrated by Henry Cole

KATHERINE TEGEN BOOKS
An Imprint of HarperCollinsPublishers

Gigi and Lulu did everything together.

If Gigi dressed in her pink striped overalls, Lulu did, too.

"You're like two little candy canes," said Lulu's grandma.

Every day they brought peanut butter sandwiches for lunch.

"You're like two little squirrels," said Gigi's dad.

When Gigi twisted a blue bow around her curly tail, Lulu
tied a blue bow on her long tail.

"Like two little blue butterflies," said Lulu's mom.

Every Wednesday without fail Gigi and Lulu wore their absolutely-the-same green sneakers with spotted yellow laces.

"You're like two peas in a pod," said Gigi and Lulu's teacher.

Then one day Gigi and Lulu had a *gigantic fight*!
"You knocked over my block house," said Lulu.
"No, I didn't," said Gigi. "You put it in my way."
"I'm never going to speak to you again," declared Lulu.
"I don't care!" yelled Gigi. "Because I'm never going to speak to you again either."

"You're being silly," said Gigi's dad. "Lulu is your best friend."
"No, she is not!" said Gigi.

"You're being silly," said Lulu's mom. "Gigi is your best friend."
"No, she is not!" said Lulu.

"Give each other a hug and make up," said Gigi and Lulu's teacher.

"Won't!" said Gigi.

"Won't!" said Lulu.

Lulu played jump rope at one
end of the playground.

Gigi climbed on the jungle gym
at the other end.

Oo Pp Qq Rr Ss Tt Uu Vv W

On Tuesday, Gigi and Lulu's teacher had some exciting news.

"I want each of you to choose a special person. Tomorrow you may dress alike, bring the same things for lunch, and work together in class. Tomorrow is Twin Day!"

"Yay!" cried everyone in the class except Gigi and Lulu.

Lulu stuck her nose in the air. "I'm not doing it," she said. "I don't know a special person."

Gigi turned her back on Lulu. "I don't know a special person either," she said.

"Never mind," said their teacher. "Why don't you just dress in the clothes you like best and bring your own favorite things for lunch?"

"Okay," said Gigi.
"Okay," said Lulu.

That evening Lulu searched through her closet for her very favorite clothes. She packed her lunch box with her very favorite things to eat.

Gigi already knew what she wanted to wear. She packed
her lunch box before she went to bed.

When Gigi and Lulu arrived in class everyone was excited.
James and Lizzie had bandanas tied around their heads.
Alex and Henry wore polka-dot shirts, like clowns.

Jack and Nick had on cowboy hats. "Howdy, partner," called Jack.

Everyone laughed and giggled. Everyone except Gigi and Lulu.

Lulu took off her coat and hung it on her peg.

"Oh!" said Gigi. "I thought you liked your pink striped overalls best of all."

"No," said Lulu. "I like my red velvet dress."

Gigi took off her coat and hung it on her peg.

"Oh!" said Lulu. "I thought you liked *your* pink striped overalls best of all."

"No," said Gigi. "I'd rather have my orange jumpsuit."

"What have you brought for lunch?" asked Lulu.

"Pickle and lettuce sandwiches," said Gigi. "What have you got?"

"Yogurt and potato chips," said Lulu.

"Oh!" said Gigi. "I don't like yogurt."

"I don't like pickles," said Lulu.

"I thought you'd wear your blue bow," said Lulu.

"I'd rather have purple," said Gigi. "I thought you'd wear *your* blue bow."

"I don't really like bows," said Lulu. "They come untied all the time."

Gigi looked at Lulu. "We didn't choose one single thing the same," she said.

"Yes, we did," said Lulu. "It's Wednesday, so we've both got on our absolutely-the-same green sneakers with spotted yellow laces."

"They're my very favorite," cried Gigi.

"They're my very favorite, too," cried Lulu.

"We do like some things the same," said Gigi. "But we like lots of things different. I guess we're not like two little peas in a pod after all."

"No," said Lulu. "But I think that's okay. Now we can just be Gigi and Lulu...

"BEST FRIENDS."

For Bernice (Bowskill) Burgess,

my "best friend" at school! With love,

P.D.E.

To Wendy Linda Bambi, with love,

H.C.

Gigi and Lulu's Gigantic Fight
Text copyright © 2004 by Pamela Duncan Edwards
Illustrations copyright © 2004 by Henry Cole
Manufactured in China by South China Printing Company Ltd.
All rights reserved.
www.harperchildrens.com

Library of Congress Cataloging-in-Publication Data
Edwards, Pamela Duncan.
  Gigi and Lulu's gigantic fight / by Pamela Duncan Edwards ; illustrated by Henry
Cole.—1st ed.
      p. cm.
Summary: After a falling out, best friends Gigi and Lulu discover that, while it can be
fun to do the same things most of the time, sometimes it is good to be different.
  ISBN 0-06-050752-7 — ISBN 0-06-050753-5 (lib. bdg.)
  [1. Identity—Fiction. 2. Best friends—Fiction. 3. Friendship—Fiction. 4. Schools—
Fiction.] I. Cole, Henry, ill. II. Title.
PZ7.E26365 Gi 2004 [E]—dc21
2003012647

Typography by Elynn Cohen   1 2 3 4 5 6 7 8 9 10   ❖   First Edition